DISCOVERING PLANTS AND ANIMALS

Science Activities and Worksheets for Young Children

by Rosie Seaman

Fearon Teacher Aids
a division of
David S. Lake Publishers
Belmont, California

About the Author

Rosie Soto Seaman is well known along the Gulf Coast as an author, educator, and television producer. She is the Director of Children's Programming for WKRG-TV in Mobile, Alabama. She has been involved with *Rosie's Place, Small Fry News,* and *Youth Magazine,* three long-running, award-winning children's programs. Rosie has also received regional acclaim for her art, early childhood, and special education courses.

Illustrated by Duane Bibby

ISBN 0-8224-1928-9

Printed in the United States of America

1. 9 8 7 6 5 4 3 2

Half Price Books
1835 Forms Drive
Carrollton, TX 75006
OFS OrderID 38623820

Thank you for your order, Main Address!

Thank you for shopping with Half Price Books! Please contact Support@hpb.com. if you have any questions, comments or concerns about your order (113-4619157-5409052)

Visit our stores to sell your books, music, movies games for cash.

SKU	ISBN/UPC	Title & Author/Artist	Shelf ID	Qty	OrderSKU
S468677646	9780822419280	Discovering Plants and Animals Seaman, Rosie	DB 30.12.4	1	

SHIPPED STANDARD TO:
Main Address
800 Avondale Ave
1033648-1-0109
Grandview Heights OH 43212
j1gg094j97htty5@marketplace.amazon.com

ORDER# **113-4619157-5409052**
AmazonMarketplaceUS

Contents

Teacher's Guide

These Are Plants, page 7

Concept: Living things can be divided into two categories—plants and animals.

Lesson: Bring several plants to class and let the children tell about plants they have at home or can see at school. Name some plants for the children—grass, trees, flowers, bushes. Use the worksheet to reinforce children's understanding of the concept.

Most Plants Are Green, page 8

Concept: There are many kinds of plants, but most of them are green.

Lesson: On a neighborhood walk, ask children to notice the plants and how they are different. Reinforce the concept that most plants are green. Use the worksheet to underscore this idea.

There Are Many Kinds of Plants, page 9

Concept: Plants have many sizes and shapes.

Lesson: Use pictures from magazines to show different kinds of plants. Ask children to name some plants they know. Use the worksheet to reinforce the ideas that plants look different and are different sizes.

Plants Can Grow, page 10

Concept: Plants are alive and grow.

Lesson: Allow children to observe the process of plant growth with seedlings in small cups. Let the children measure the plants' growth over the period of several weeks. Use the worksheet to reinforce the sequence of growth in plants.

Plants Need Light, page 11

Concept: Plants need light to grow.

Lesson: Use two seedlings in small paper cups. Put one in a lighted area and the other in a dark place such as a closet. Let the children observe the progress of the plants after a few days. Point out to the children that both plants have had water. Use the worksheet to reinforce the concept.

Plants Need Light and Water, page 12

Concept: Plants need both light and water to grow.

Lesson: Let children participate in the following experiment with three seedlings. Give one water but no light; give one light but no water; and give one both light and water. Help children formulate the idea that plants need both light and water to grow. Use the worksheet to reinforce this concept.

These Are Plant Parts, page 13

Concept: Most plants have a root system, leaves, and stems.

Lesson: Point out the parts of plants to the children. Use a house plant to demonstrate the system of roots. Explain how the roots take water and nutrients from the soil and how the leaves take energy from the sun. Use the worksheet to reinforce the concept.

Some Plants Have Flowers, page 14

Concept: Many plants produce flowers in their reproductive cycle.

Lesson: Help children understand that flowers are a stage in the reproductive cycle of many plants. Demonstrate that flowers contain seeds or that flowers become fruits that contain seeds. Use a sunflower and let children shake out the seeds. Use the worksheet to reinforce the concept of plants with flowers.

Some Plants Grow Fruits, page 15

Concept: Plants produce fruits that contain seeds. (We like to eat many of these fruits.)

Lesson: Let children name some fruits. Show them pictures of plants bearing fruits. Stress the ideas that each plant produces fruits of one kind and that fruits contain seeds. Use the worksheet to reinforce the concept that each plant produces a fruit that is identifiable.

Fruits Have Seeds, page 16

Concept: Fruits contain different kinds of seeds.

Lesson: Bring several kinds of fruits to class. Cut them open and allow children to look at the seeds. Remove the seeds and let children group cleaned seeds into like and unlike. Cut the fruits into small pieces and serve to children at snacktime. Use the worksheet to reinforce the concepts that fruits contain seeds and that different fruits contain different seeds.

Seeds Grow into Plants, page 17

Concept: Seeds contain the materials that make new plants under growing conditions.

Lesson: Allow children to plant some seeds that germinate easily, such as lima beans. Reinforce the concept with the worksheet.

Green Plants Have Leaves, page 18

Concept: Most plants are green, and they make food in their leaves.

Lesson: Allow children to collect leaf samples either at home or during a class walk. Ask them to compare the leaves' shapes, colors, sizes, and forms. Use the worksheet to reinforce the concept that leaves come in different shapes and can be used to help us identify plants.

This Is a Tree, page 19

Concept: All trees have common characteristics.

Lesson: Show the children pictures of different kinds of trees. Help them discover what the trees have in common—leaves, branches, trunk (bark), and a root system. Take the children on a walk to compare different trees. Use the worksheet to reinforce the concepts.

Kinds of Trees, page 20

Concept: There are trees with small needle leaves that stay green, and trees with broad leaves that lose their leaves.

Lesson: Show pictures of the two kinds of trees. Show pictures of deciduous trees with their leaves changing colors and when all the leaves have fallen. Use the worksheet to reinforce the ideas.

Trees Are Useful, page 21

Concept: Trees are the source of many things that are important to human life—wood products, food, paper products, as well as the oxygen we breathe.

Lesson: Make a poster or mural with the children. Let them use magazines to find pictures of the things made from trees. Ask the children to cut these items out and help them paste the pictures onto the poster. Label the poster: We Need Trees. Use the worksheet to reinforce the importance of trees in our lives.

These Are Animals, page 22

Concept: There are many kinds of animals that differ from each other and from other living and nonliving objects.

Lesson: Show children pictures of animals, plants, and nonliving objects. Let them distinguish between the categories. Discuss the attributes that help us to decide whether something is alive, and whether it is a plant or an animal. Use the worksheet to reinforce the concept of what an animal is.

Most Baby Animals Look Like Their Parents, page 23

Concept: Most animals reproduce offspring that resemble them immediately. (Other animals' offspring will go through stages before they are like the parents.)

Lesson: Show pictures of animals with young. Point out the resemblances between parents and offspring. Talk about how the parents care for the young. Use the worksheet to reinforce the concept that offspring can resemble their parents.

Some Baby Animals Grow Up to Look Like Their Parents, page 24

Concept: The young of some animals go through stages of growth before looking like the parents.

Lesson: Allow children to observe the changes in tadpoles if you have access to an aquarium. If not, use pictures to show this progress. Moths are also interesting animals to observe, but the cycle is long. (The concept story "The Little Brown Cradle," from *Paper Stories* by Jean Stangl published by David S. Lake Publishers, helps to get the moth's story across to children.) Use the worksheet to reinforce the concept of developmental stages.

Some Baby Animals Are Hatched, page 25

Concept: Some animals lay eggs that contain developing animals. Most of these animals tend their eggs and then their babies.

Lesson: If you have a brooder, allow children to observe the hatching of chicken eggs. Break open a regular unhatched egg to show the different parts—the shell, the white, and the yolk. Show pictures of other animal eggs and the hatched offspring. Use the worksheet to reinforce the concept.

Some Baby Animals Are Born, page 26

Concept: Some animals give birth to offspring that are ready to move about and begin eating.

Lesson: Show pictures of various identifiable mammals with their offspring. Let children tell about their pets' babies. Stress that these offspring are ready to move about soon after birth, and that their parents take care of them until they are bigger. Use the worksheet to reinforce the concepts.

Fur or Feathers? page 27

Concept: Animals have different kinds of protective coverings.

Lesson: Let children examine different kinds of feathers and samples of furs. Help them discover that each kind of covering offers protection to the animal. Use the worksheet to reinforce the concept.

Some Animals Can Fly, page 28

Concept: One way to classify animals is by how they move about. Many animals that fly are birds; most birds can fly. Exceptions are bats (flying mammals), some insects, and ostriches (flightless birds).

Lesson: Let children discover that most animals that fly are birds. Talk about the qualities that enable birds to fly (bone structures, wings, and feathers). Use the worksheet to reinforce the concepts.

Animals Can Move, page 29

Concept: Animals move about to find food and shelter in different ways.

Lesson: Show pictures of animals and discuss how they move about. Talk about the structures of the animals and how these structures allow the animals to move in particular environments. Use the worksheet to reinforce the concepts.

Animals Live in Many Places, page 30

Concept: Animals are found in every habitable place on earth. These habitats vary.

Lesson: Talk about different environments, such as the jungle, forests, lakes and oceans, and grasslands. Help the children discover that animals live in these environments and that their bodies and habits are adapted to the environments. Use the worksheet to reinforce the concepts.

Animals Build Homes, page 31

Concept: Many animals construct homes for protection.

Lesson: Show pictures of different animals' homes. Tell the children how the animals construct these homes. Help them discover the functions of homes—protection from enemies, warmth, aids in getting food, places to raise young. Use the worksheet to reinforce the concepts.

Help the Bird Go Home, page 32

Concept: Each animal constructs a special kind of home to meet its needs.

Lesson: Discuss the types of animal homes and how these homes meet the special needs of the animals. Use the worksheet to reinforce the concepts.

Big or Small? page 33

Concept: The sizes of animals vary greatly.

Lesson: Show pictures of wild animals that will give children a realistic concept of their relative sizes. Let the children discuss the biggest and smallest animals they have seen. Talk about the amounts of food each size of animal needs. Use the worksheet to reinforce the concepts.

Elephants Are Big, page 34

Concept: Elephants are the largest land animals.

Lesson: Bring a picture of an elephant that compares it to other animals. Let the children tell about seeing elephants at zoos or circuses. Talk about the elephant's habitat and eating habits. Use the worksheet to reinforce the concepts.

The Giraffe Is Tall, page 35

Concept: The giraffe is the tallest land animal.

Lesson: Use a picture to illustrate the height of this animal. Talk about its habitat and eating habits. Use the worksheet to reinforce the concepts.

Big Bird, page 36

Concept: The ostrich is the largest bird.

Lesson: Show pictures that illustrate the comparative sizes of various birds and their eggs. Tell the children that the ostrich cannot fly but is a very fast runner. Help the children discover why the ostrich is a bird even though it cannot fly. Use the worksheet to reinforce the concepts.

The Biggest Animal, page 37

Concept: Whales are large animals. The largest whale is the largest living animal.

Lesson: Show children pictures of different kinds of whales that illustrate their comparative sizes. Talk about the habits of whales, and explain why they are not fish. Let children share any experiences they have had with whales. Use the worksheet to reinforce the concepts.

These Are Some Mammals, page 38

Concept: Some animals are called mammals. Mammals give birth to their young and have milk to feed them.

Lesson: Show pictures of mammals and offspring. Explain how mammals are different from other animals—fur, live offspring, milk glands. Use the worksheet to reinforce the concepts.

These Are Some Reptiles, page 39

Concept: Reptiles are another classification of animals. They need the sun to maintain body temperature, and they have scaly skins.

Lesson: Show pictures of many different kinds of reptiles—lizards, snakes, turtles, crocodiles. Point out how they are similar and how they are different. Let the children share their experiences with different kinds of reptiles. Use the worksheet to reinforce the concepts.

These Are Some Insects, page 40

Concept: There are many kinds of insects. Most insects have six legs, three parts to their bodies, antennae, and wings at some stage of life.

Lesson: Show pictures of many kinds of insects. Let the children name some animals that are insects. Point out the parts of insects. Talk about how some insects help humans and how some are harmful. Use the worksheet to reinforce the concepts.

Parts of an Insect, page 41

Concept: Most insects have six legs, three parts to their bodies, antennae, and wings.

Lesson: Examine the parts of insects using pictures that call out the significant parts. Use the worksheet to reinforce these concepts.

Farm Animals, page 42

Concept: Some animals are raised on farms to produce food and clothing for us.

Lesson: If possible, arrange for a visit to a working farm or dairy. Let children think of all the animals they know that are raised on farms. Let them list the products these farm animals provide. Use the worksheet to reinforce the concepts.

All Animals Need Food and Water, page 43

Concept: Animals need food and water to live. Animals have different food habits and ways of getting food.

Lesson: Allow the children to discuss their own food preferences. Show them that animals also have food habits, and that their behaviors and environments play important roles in getting food. Use the worksheet to reinforce the concepts.

Some Animals Are Good Pets, page 44

Concept: Some animals are domesticated and make good pets.

Lesson: Help the children discover the characteristics that make animals good pets—size, disposition, food habits, and the like. Let the children share information about pets they have at home and tell why they are suitable pets. Lead them to discover that some animals are not suitable pets. Use the worksheet to reinforce these concepts.

Name ______________________________

These Are Plants

Color the pictures. Circle the plants.

Name ______________________________

Most Plants Are Green

Find the plants. Color them green. Color the other pictures.

Name ____________________________

There Are Many Kinds of Plants

Look at the plants. Color them green.

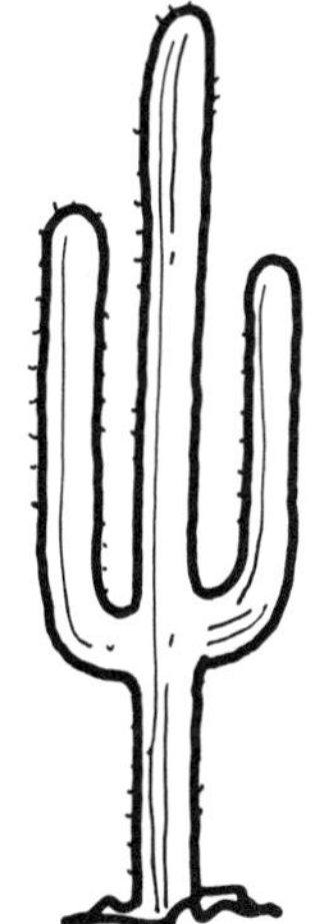

Name ______________________________

Plants Can Grow

Color the pictures. Cut and then paste the pictures to show how plants grow.

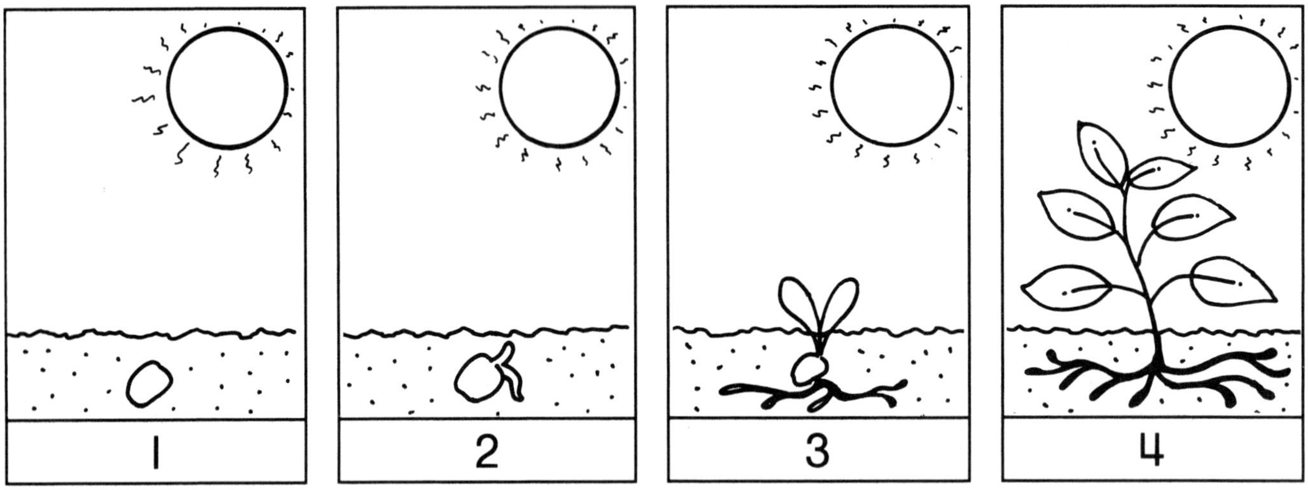

1	2	3	4

1	2	3	4

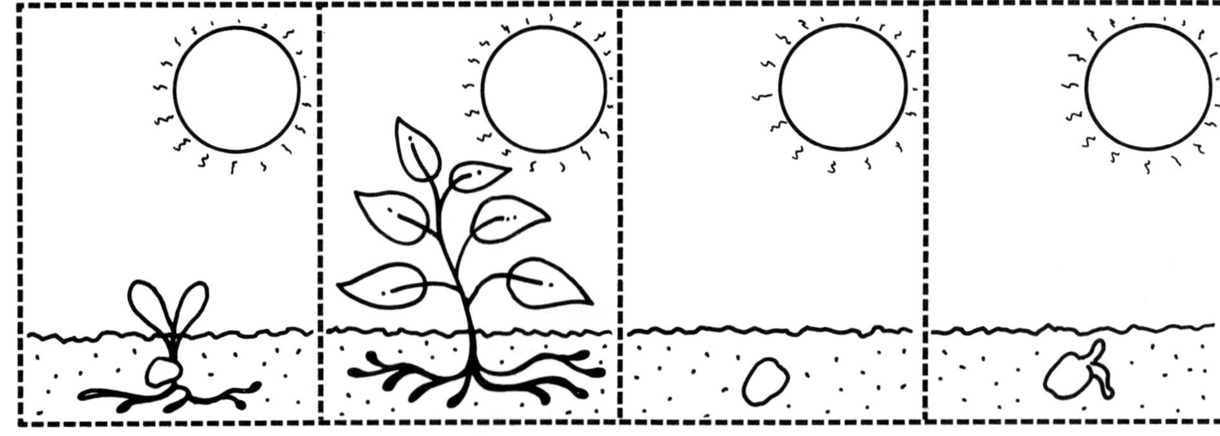

Name ______________________________

Plants Need Light

Color the pictures. Cut and then paste the pictures in the correct boxes. Trace the words.

light

no light

Name ______________________

Plants Need Light and Water

Look at each pair of pictures. Something is missing in one picture. Draw it in the correct place. Color the pictures. Trace the words.

Plants need light.

Plants need water.

Name ______________________________

These Are Plant Parts

Color the pictures. Cut and then paste the plant parts to match the plant. Trace the words.

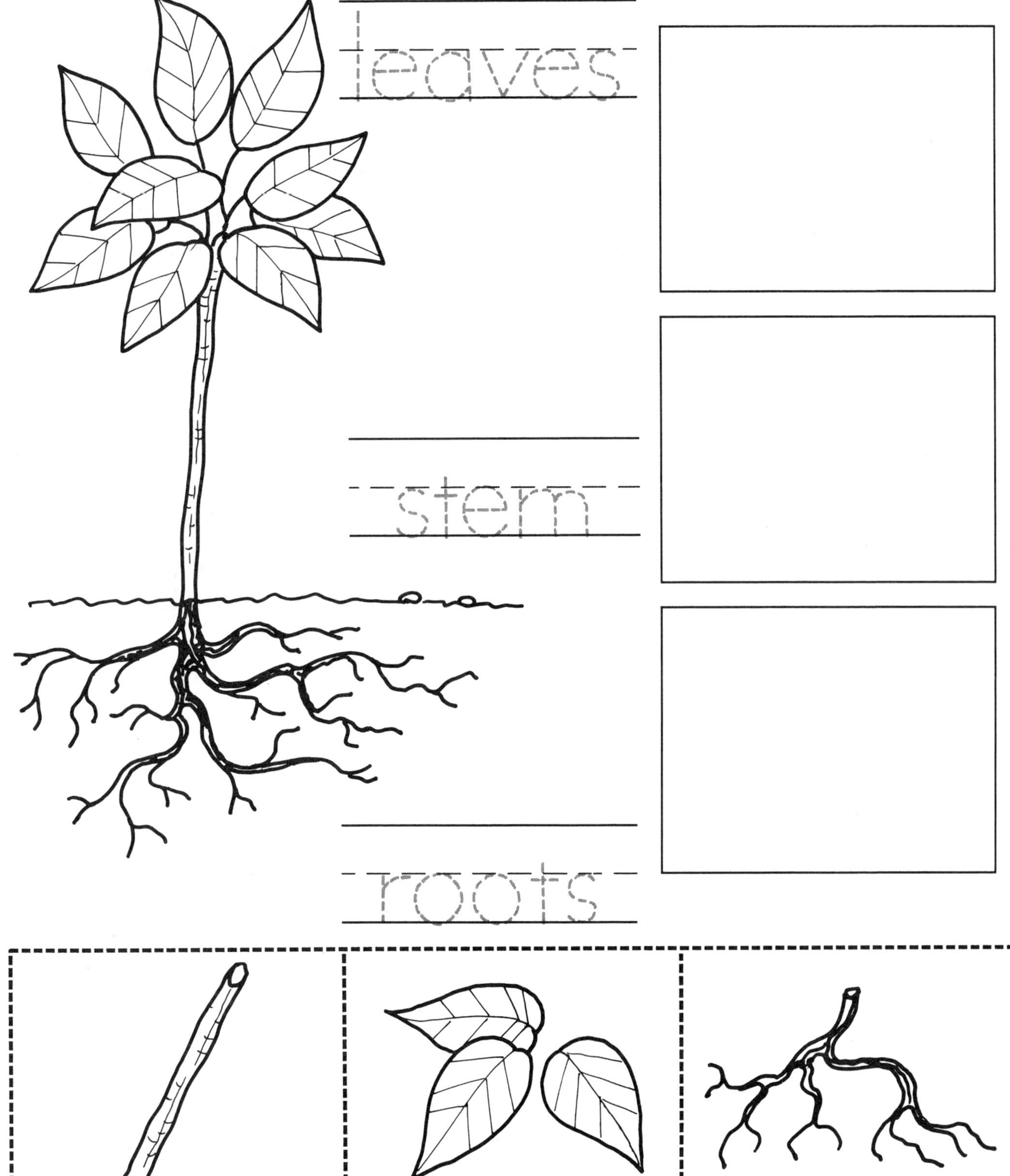

Name ______________________________

Some Plants Have Flowers

Find the plants that have flowers. Color the flowers. Color all the plants' leaves and stems green.

Name ____________________

Some Plants Grow Fruits

Color the pictures. Cut and then paste the pictures of fruits beside the correct plants.

Name ________________________________

Fruits Have Seeds

Some fruits have many small seeds. Some have one big seed. Color the pictures. Circle the fruits with one big seed.

Name ______________________________

Seeds Grow into Plants

Color the pictures. In each row something is missing. Cut and then paste to finish each row.

Name ______________________________

Green Plants Have Leaves

Look at each row. One leaf is different. Circle it. Color the leaves green.

Name ______________________________

This Is a Tree

Color the parts of the tree. Trace the words.

tree

Name ______________________________

Kinds of Trees

Complete the drawing of each tree. Color the trees. Trace the words.

pine tree

oak tree

Name ______________________________

Trees Are Useful

Look at the pictures. Find the things we get from trees. Color them.

Name ______________________________

These Are Animals

Circle the animals in each row. Color them.

Name ______________________________

Most Baby Animals Look Like Their Parents

Color the pictures. Draw a line to match each baby with its parent.

Name ______________________________

Some Baby Animals Grow Up to Look Like Their Parents

Color the pictures. Draw a line to match each baby animal with its parent. Circle the babies who look like their parents.

Name ____________________

Some Baby Animals Are Hatched

Draw a line to match each baby animal with its parent. Color the pictures.

Name ______________________________

Some Baby Animals Are Born

Cut and then paste the pictures of baby animals to show which are born and which are hatched. Match each baby to its parent. Color the pictures.

Born		Hatched	

Name ______________________________

Fur or Feathers?

Some animals have feathers. Some animals have fur. Cut and then paste the pictures of animals in the correct places. Trace the words. Color the pictures.

Name ______________________________

Some Animals Can Fly

In each row, circle the animal that can fly. Color the pictures. Trace the words.

Some animals have wings.

Name ______________________________

Animals Can Move

Look at the pictures of animals. Color the pictures. Cut and then paste the pictures to show how the animals move.

Crawl	Walk	Swim	Fly

Name ______________________________

Animals Live in Many Places

Color the pictures. Cut and then paste the pictures of animals to show where they live.

Name ______________________

Animals Build Homes

Color the pictures. Cut and then paste the pictures to show each animal's home.

Name ______________________________

Help the Bird Go Home

Color the picture. Draw a line through the maze to help the bird go home.

Name ______________________________

Big or Small?

Look at each picture. Circle the animal that is bigger. Color the pictures. Trace the words.

big or small

Name ______________________________

Elephants Are Big

Color the pictures of the animals. Cut and then paste to show the sizes of the animals. Trace the words.

big bigger biggest

Name ______________________________

The Giraffe Is Tall

Color the picture. Trace the words.

a tall giraffe

Name ______________________________

Big Bird

Follow the dots to complete the picture. Color the picture. Trace the words.

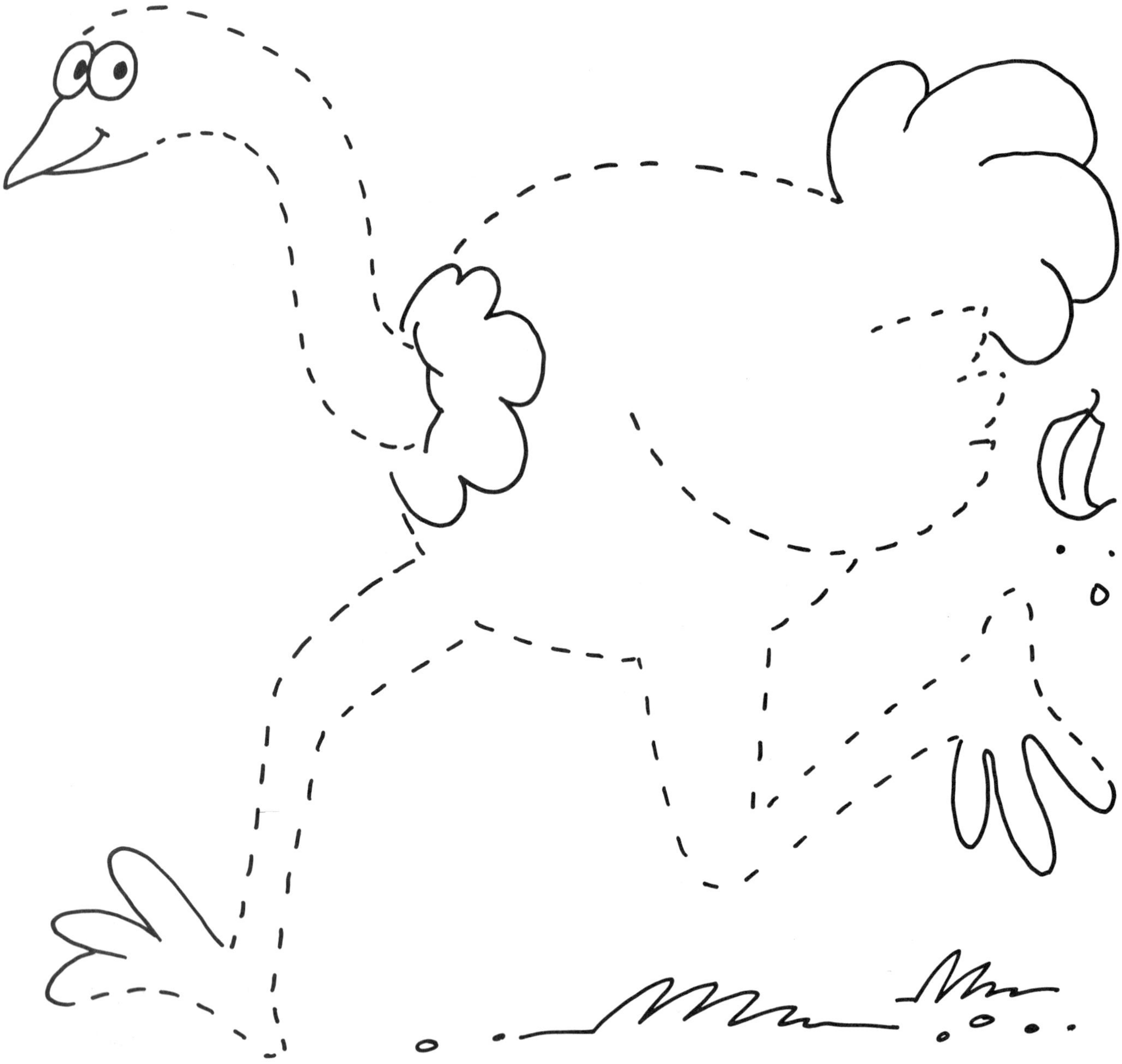

Discovering Plants and Animals, © 1987 David S. Lake Publishers

An ostrich can run.

Name ________________________________

The Biggest Animal

Color the pictures. Cut and then paste the picture of the whale. Trace the words.

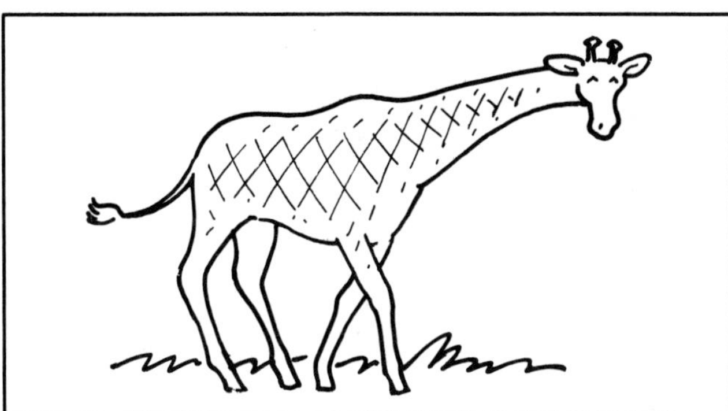

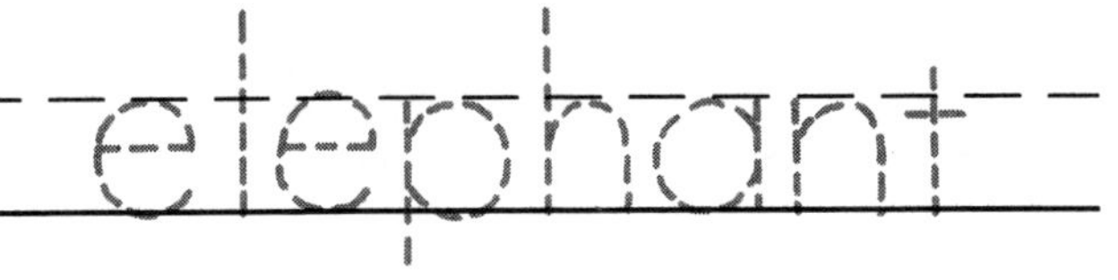

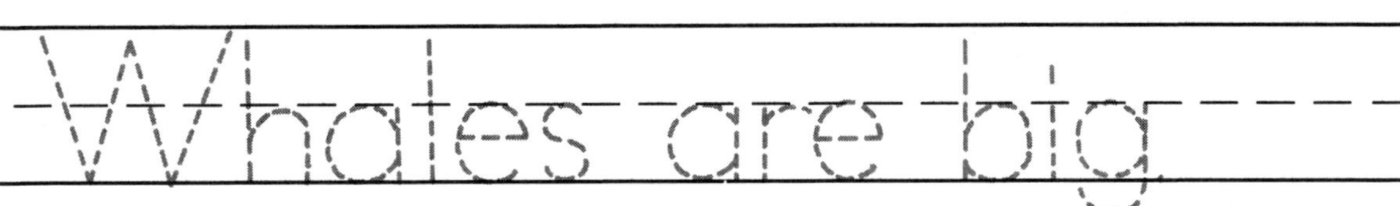

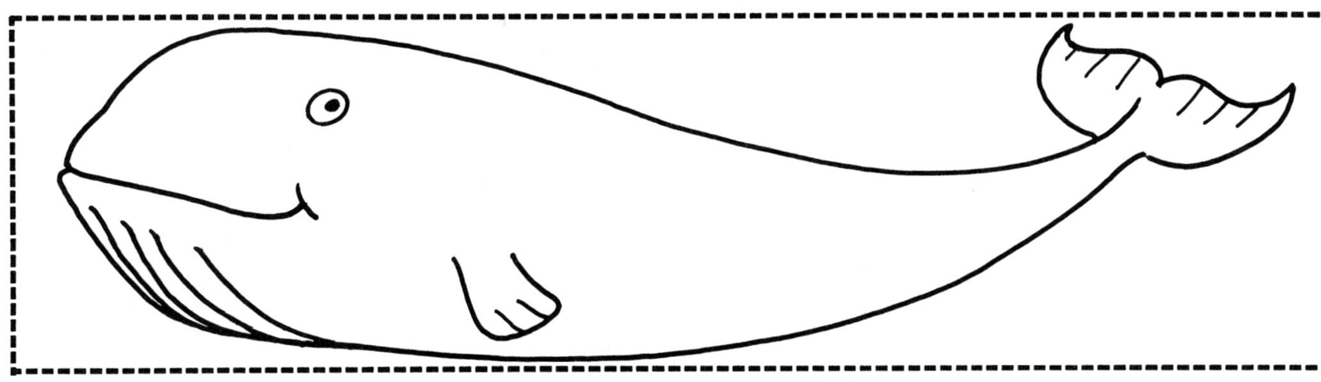

Name ______________________________

These Are Some Mammals

Color the pictures. Cut and then paste on the big picture only the pictures of mammals.

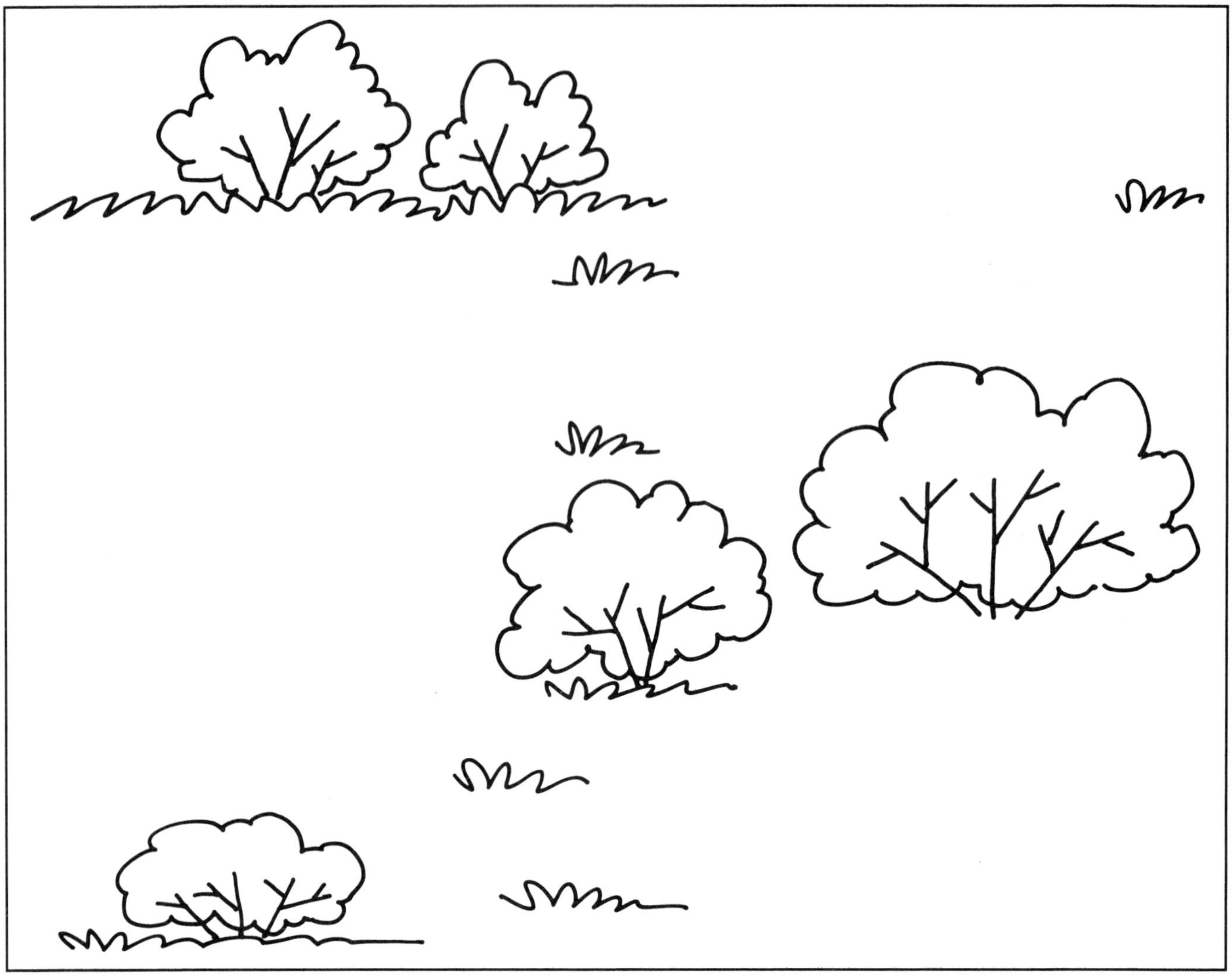

Name ______________________________

These Are Some Reptiles

Color the pictures. Cut and then paste on the big picture only the pictures of reptiles.

Name ______________________________

These Are Some Insects

Color the pictures. Cut and then paste on the big picture only the pictures of insects.

Name ______________________

Parts of an Insect

Color the picture. Trace the words.

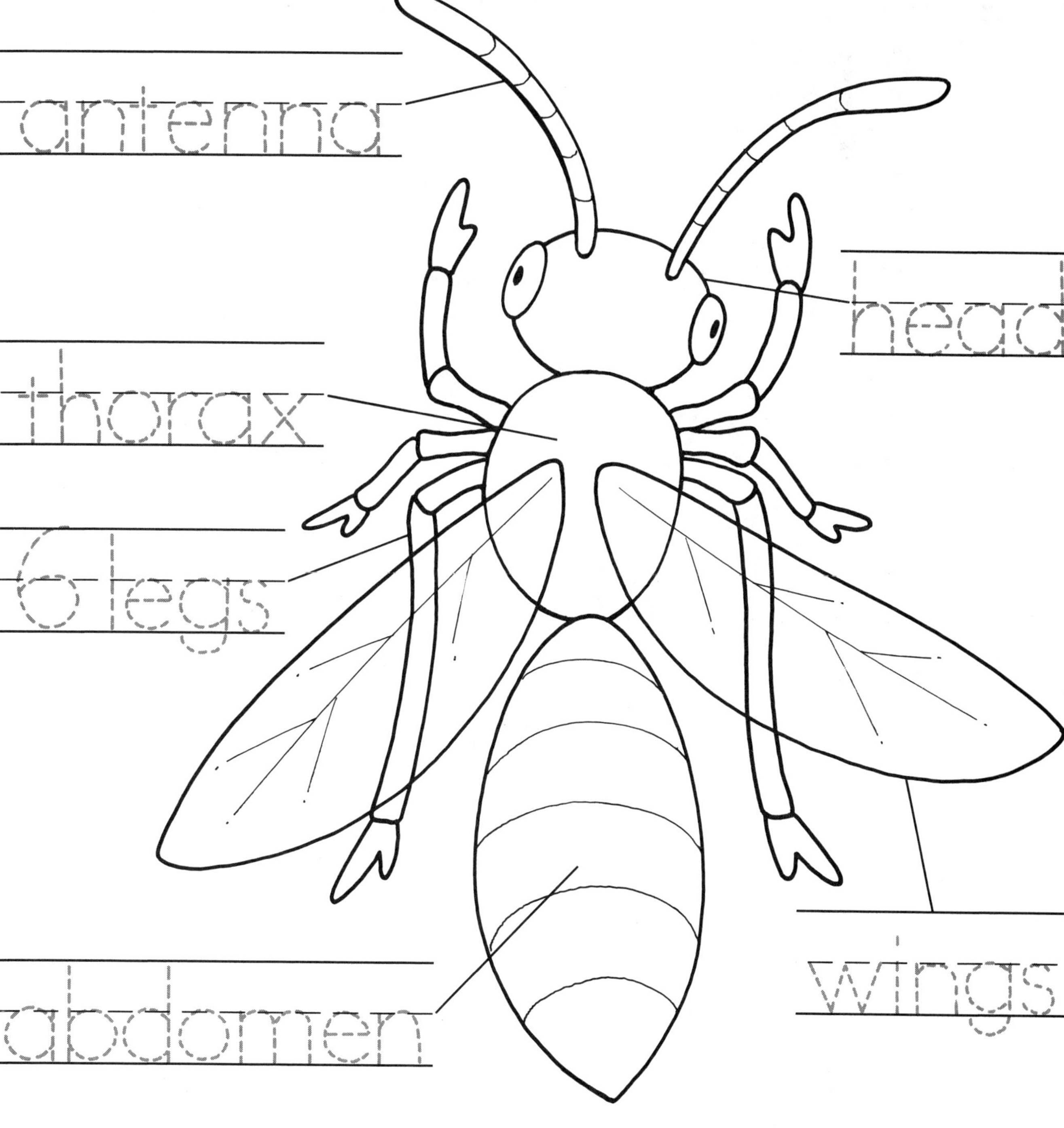

A bee is an insect.

Farm Animals

Color the pictures. In each row, circle the animal that does not belong on a farm.

Name ______________________________

All Animals Need Food and Water

Color the pictures. Cut and then paste the picture of each food beside the animal that eats it. Trace the words.

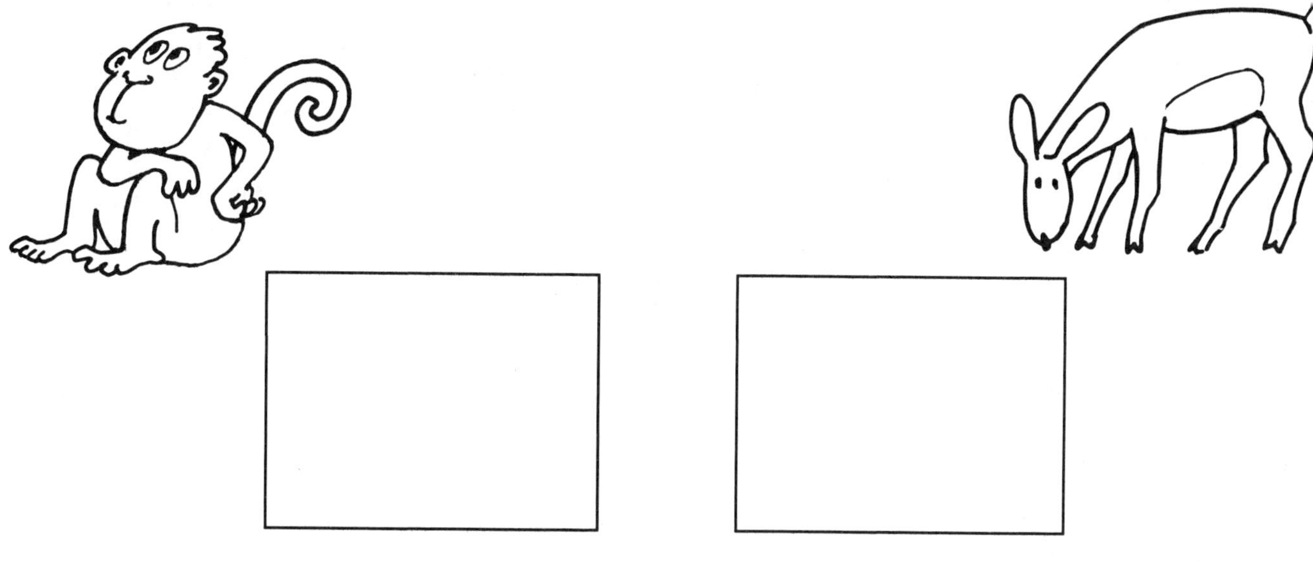

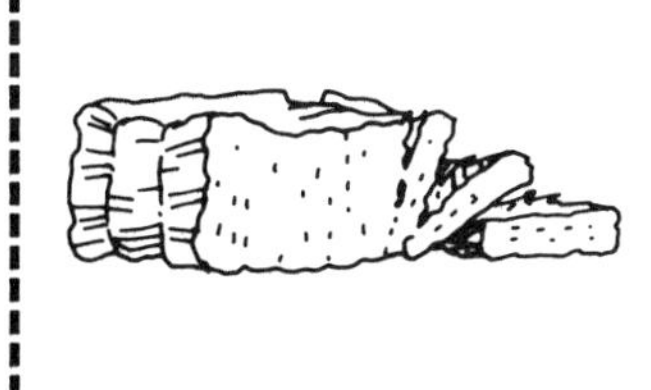

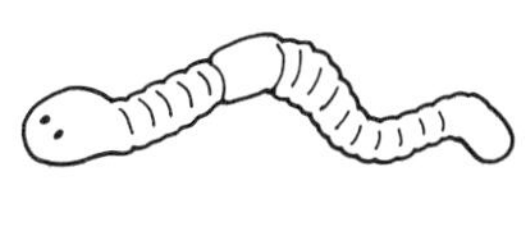

Name ______________________________

Some Animals Are Good Pets

Trace the dotted lines to complete the picture. Color the picture.
Trace the words.